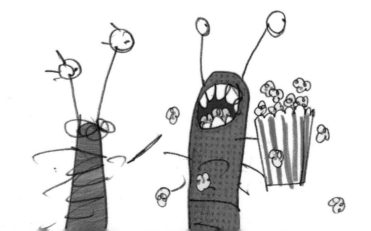

You Can't take an Elephant on the Bus

Patricia Cleveland-Peck

Illustrated by David Tazzyman

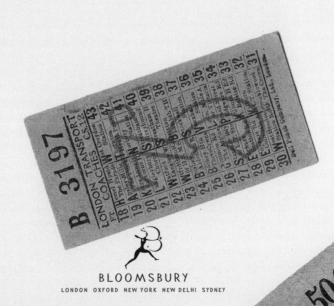

BLOOMSBURY

LONDON OXFORD NEW YORK NEW DELHI SYDNEY

You can't take an **elephant** on the **bus** . . .

It would simply cause a terrible fuss!
Elephants' bottoms are heavy and fat,
and would certainly squash the seats quite flat.

And don't sit a **monkey** in a **shopping trolley**...

For monkeys are naughty and find it jolly
to snatch your shopping and chuck it about.
No, leave monkey at home when you go out.

Nor should a **tiger** travel by **train** . . .

Think of the panic. Think of the pain.
Tigers are built to spring and to leap.
Think of the passengers half-asleep.

And don't hail a **taxi** if the driver's a **seal** . . .

With such slippery flippers, he can't grasp the wheel.
The taxi will slither and probably swerve,
then throw everyone out at the very next curve.

A **centipede** on roller skates is rather bizarre . . .

With one hundred feet, he'd go fast and go far.
But to put on his boots would take him an age –
he'd get in a temper, he'd get in a rage.

And don't put a **camel** in a **sailing boat** . . .

It's far too tricky to keep afloat.
His hump and his feet would, I think,
capsize the vessel
and
make it
sink.

A **giraffe** in an **aeroplane** wouldn't be right . . .

The roof of a plane just hasn't the height.
With legs and a neck so bony and long,
a giraffe on a plane would simply be wrong.

And don't ask a **whale** to ride a **bike** . . .

Just imagine what it would be like –
without a bottom to sit on the seat.
And how would he pedal without any feet?

A **pig** on a skateboard? Another mistake . . .

He'd be too heavy, it would probably break.
Or his trotters would totter, unable to grip,
and up-and-over the skateboard would flip.

And I wouldn't put a **hippo** in a **hot air balloon**...

The basket's too small, there wouldn't be room.
And if it did fly, with hippo's great weight,
it would come crashing down in a terrible state.

And never let a **bear** near an **ice cream van** . . .

Bears gobble up ice cream as fast as they can.
And if they're stopped they get annoyed,
and an angry bear is one best to avoid.

"Then how can we travel?"
the animals shout.
"How can we animals get carried about?"

"What's the best vehicle?
We haven't a clue."

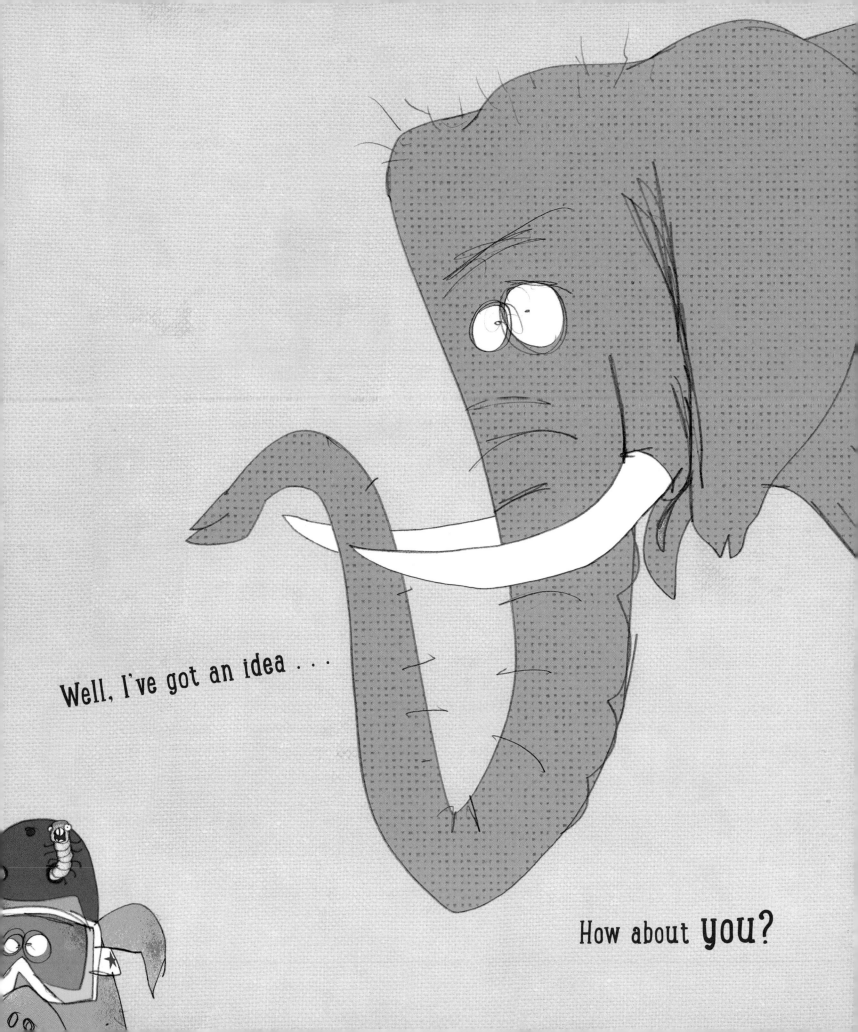

Well, I've got an idea . . .

How about **you?**

Yes, **animals** on **rollercoasters** are good for a laugh . . .

There's room here for EVERYONE – even giraffe!
So it's goodbye to skateboards, balloons and THAT bus,
for we now have a conveyance that suits ALL OF US!

whee

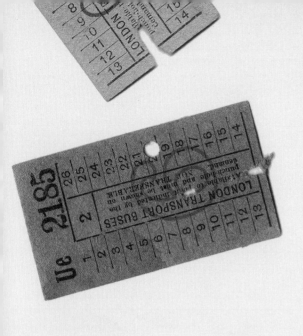

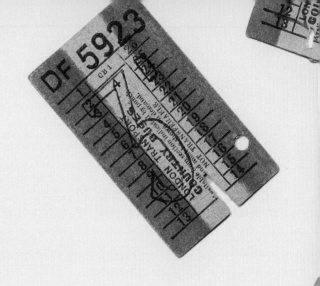

To Isabel, with love ~ PC-P

For Mum and Dad x ~ DT

Bloomsbury Publishing, London, Oxford, New York, New Delhi and Sydney

First published in Great Britain in 2015 by Bloomsbury Publishing Plc
50 Bedford Square, London WC1B 3DP

www.bloomsbury.com

BLOOMSBURY is a registered trademark of Bloomsbury Publishing Plc

Text copyright © Patricia Cleveland-Peck 2015
Illustrations copyright © David Tazzyman 2015

The moral rights of the author and illustrator have been asserted

A CIP catalogue record for this book is available from the British Library

ISBN 978 1 4088 4980 4 (HB)
ISBN 978 1 4088 4982 8 (PB)
ISBN 978 1 4088 4981 1 (eBook)

All papers used by Bloomsbury Publishing are natural, recyclable products
made from wood grown in well-managed forests.
The manufacturing processes conform to the environmental regulations of the country of origin

Printed in China by Leo Paper Products, Heshan, Guangdong

12